For Lulu, Papa, Stephanie and Mary. – AA

For Carrie (and her ukulele). – NQ

I AM NEFERTITI

First published in Great Britain in 2022 by Five Quills
93 Oakwood Court, London W14 8JZ
www.fivequills.co.uk

Five Quills and associated logos are trademarks of Five Quills Ltd.

A CIP record for this title is available from the British Library

ISBN 978-1-912923-31-1

3 5 7 9 10 8 6 4 2

Printed and Bound in the United Kingdom by Bell & Bain Ltd

I AM NEFERTITI

ANNEMARIE ANANG

NATELLE QUEK

"Have you packed your drumsticks, Nefertiti?"

"Yes, Dad!" said Nefertiti. "Do you really think I'm ready?"

"Of course! You've been playing drums since you were little. You are ready."

"You're right, Dad. I *am* ready."

Nefertiti looked up nervously at the music building.
"This is where the band rehearses," said Dad. "Go in,
play those drums, and always remember: *You are Nefertiti.*"

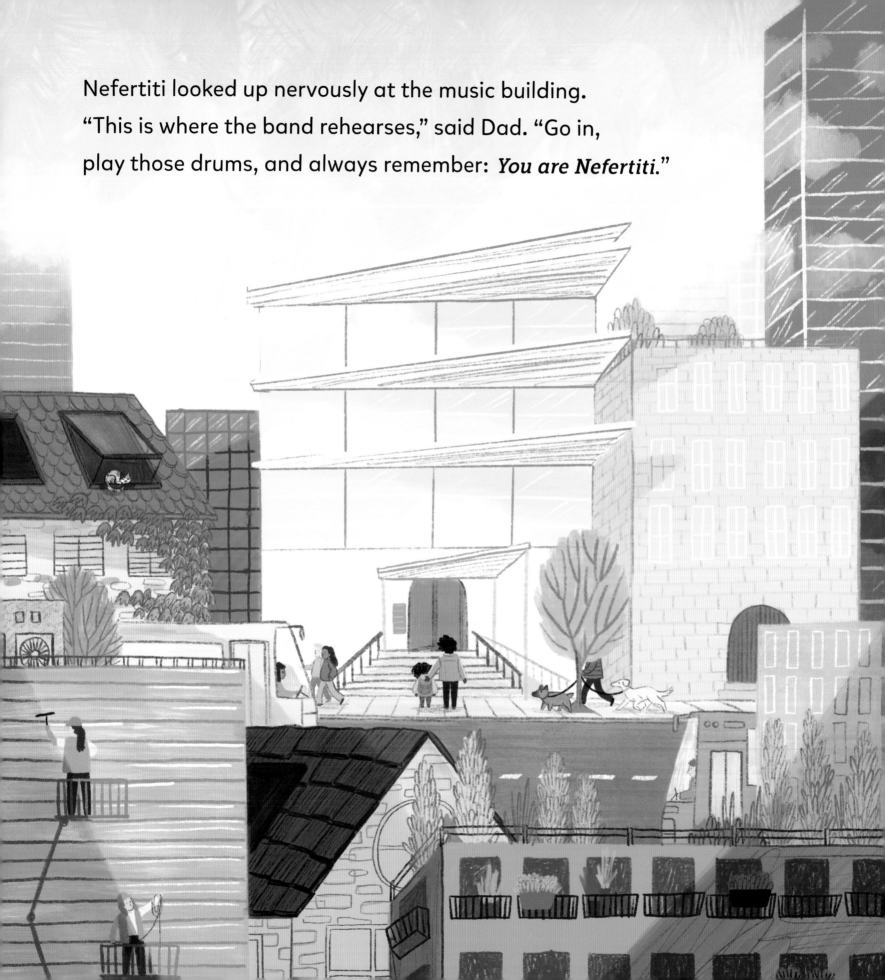

Dad always said *'You are Nefertiti'* when she felt nervous,
and it made her feel ten feet tall.
"*I am Nefertiti*," she whispered.

"Are you the new drummer?" asked the teacher, excitedly.

"Yes, I am," answered Nefertiti.

"Welcome! Let me introduce you to the band:

Kofi plays recorder.

Kai plays kalimba.

Pippa's on piano.

Priya plays marimba.

Josh plays violin.

Joy's on ukulele."

"I'm Miss Potts, the singer! And you are . . .?"

"I'm Nefertiti," said Nefertiti, proudly.

"Nefer-who?" asked Miss Potts.

"**Nefertiti.**"

"That's a tricky name. I'm going to call you . . . 'Nef'.
Nef will be easier for the band to say," said Miss Potts.

The strangest thing happened when Miss Potts said 'Nef'.

Nefertiti's skin *tightened up* and her body seemed to *shrink*, just a little.

I must be imagining things, thought Nefertiti.

"Children, let's play Nef our song," said Miss Potts.

"Hit it!"

Kofi's recorder squeaked.

Kai's kalimba clanged.

Pippa's piano plonked.

Priya's marimba plinked.

Josh's violin screeched.

Joy's ukulele twanged.

And Miss Potts howled, and oh, how she scowled.
Without a drummer to keep the beat,
everything sounded higgledy-piggledy.

"STOP!" Miss Potts shouted.

"Nef, give us a beat."

Nefertiti felt her skin *tighten up* and her body *shrink* again.

When she sat down to play the drums, her feet did not even touch the floor!

"Come on, Nef, give us a beat!" said Miss Potts again.

Nefertiti took a deep breath and . . .

Cu cu cha cha, Cu cu cha, Cu cu cha cha, Cu cu cha

she drummed,
and this time:

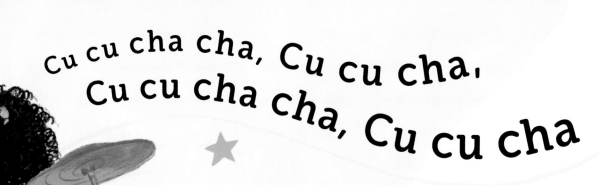

Kofi's recorder soared.

Kai's kalimba soothed.

Pippa's piano rocked.

Priya's marimba jived.

Josh's violin glided.

Joy's ukulele grooved.

And Miss Potts sang,

"Hooray! SHOO-bee-dee day!"

Everyone listened to Nefertiti's beat, and now the music sounded so sweet!

"Ohhh, yeaaah! We finally sound like a band!" laughed Miss Potts.

She chanted:

"Nef,

Nef,

Nef."

But every time she chanted 'Nef', Nefertiti shrank.

She shrank and shrank, until she was just the size of your thumb.

Nefertiti's drumsticks **c r a s h e d** onto the floor.

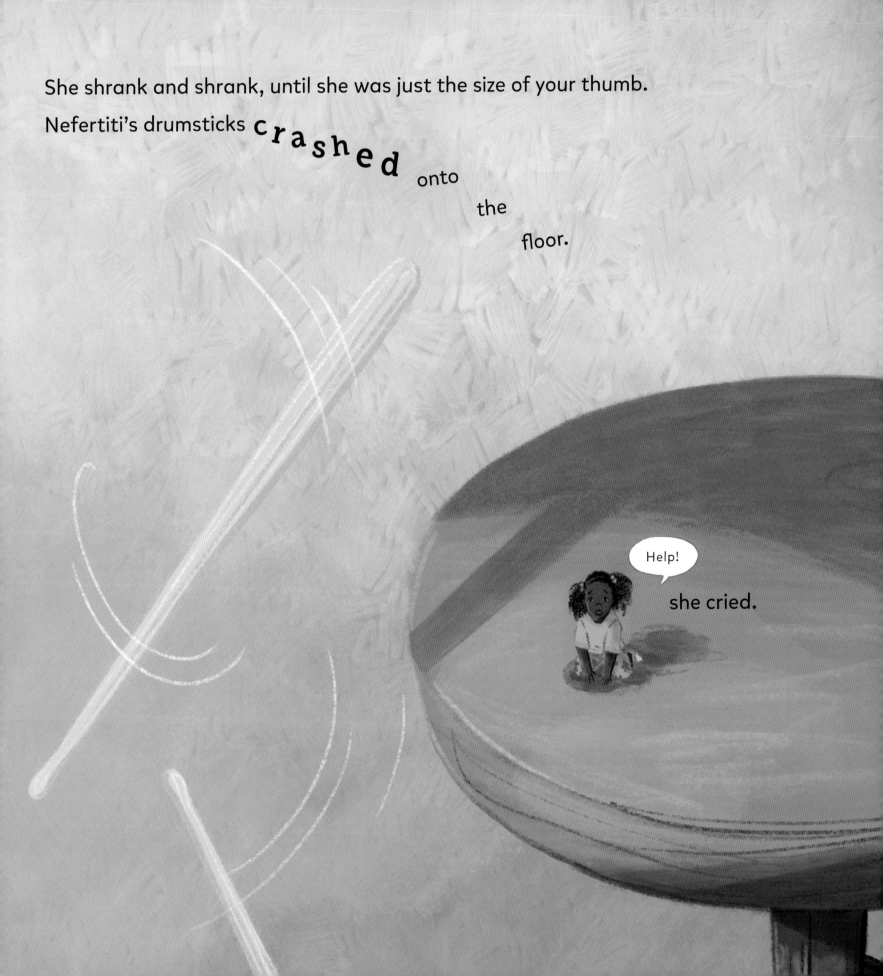

Help!

she cried.

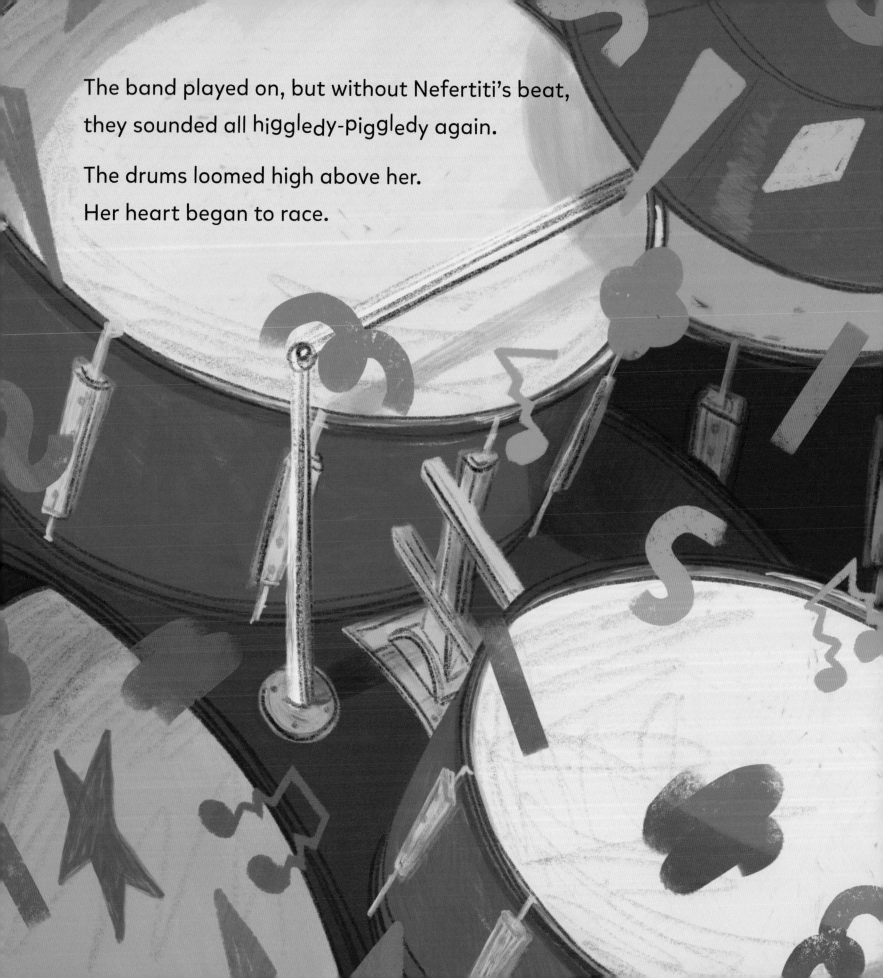

The band played on, but without Nefertiti's beat,
they sounded all higgledy-piggledy again.

The drums loomed high above her.
Her heart began to race.

Nefertiti tried not to panic.
Then she remembered her dad's words.
You are Nefertiti.

"Nef? Where's Nef?" Miss Potts shouted above the din.

I'm here, Miss Potts!

Miss Potts looked around. "Nef?"

"Look!" said Kofi. "There's a bug jumping up and down on Nefertiti's chair!"

"That's not a bug. That's Nefertiti!" said Pippa.

"**Woah!!**" gasped everyone.

Nefertiti tried to explain what had happened, but her voice was too quiet. "Wait!" said Priya.

Nefertiti climbed onto Priya's hand, and whispered what Miss Potts needed to do, to make her grow big again.

"She says she'll grow bigger if you call her by her real name," Priya said.

"Oh, goodness . . . I don't *remember* her real name," said Miss Potts.

"That's easy," said Kai. "It's Nefertiti. Like the Egyptian queen."

"OK. Let me try. **Ne-fer-tiii-tiii**," said Miss Potts, nervously.

Everyone watched and waited, but Nefertiti did not grow one bit.

"Say it like you mean it, Miss Potts!" said Joy.

"Ne-fer-ti-ti!"

said Miss Potts, more confidently.

All of a sudden, Nefertiti began to shine like the brightest star . . .

. . . and she **began** to **grow**.

"Ne-fer-ti-ti! Ne-fer-ti-ti!" everyone chanted.
And, little by little, Nefertiti grew –
until she was back to her normal size.

"Hooray, hooray, for **Nefertiti today!**" everyone cheered.

"Sorry I changed your name, Nefertiti," said Miss Potts.
"It must be wonderful to be named after an Egyptian queen."
Nefertiti nodded. "My grandma chose it for me.
It means 'a beautiful woman has come'."

"It's a lovely name." Miss Potts smiled
and handed Nefertiti her drumsticks.

Back at their places, the band waited for Nefertiti's cue.

"*I am Nefertiti*," Nefertiti whispered,

then she drummed, just like she'd done since she was little.

Cu cu cha cha, Cu cu cha,
Cu cu cha cha, Cu cu cha!

What **marvellous music** they made.